THE BOSSY PIRATE

JOHN STEVEN GURNEY

BOB

SALTY JACK

SANJAY

Library of Congress Control Number: 2018937051

Art Direction and layout by Danielle D. Farmer
Cover design by Danielle Farmer
Illustrations by John Steven Gurney
Type set in Corida New/Windlass

ISBN: 978-0-7643-5625-4
Printed in China

Published by Schiffer Publishing, Ltd.
4880 Lower Valley Road
Atglen, PA 19310
Phone: (610) 593-1777; Fax: (610) 593-2002
E-mail: Info@schifferbooks.com
Web: www.schifferbooks.com

For our complete selection of fine books on this and related subjects, please visit our website at www.schifferbooks. com. You may also write for a free catalog.

Schiffer Publishing's titles are available at special discounts for bulk purchases for sales promotions or premiums. Special editions, including personalized covers, corporate imprints, and excerpts, can be created in large quantities for special needs. For more information, contact the publisher.

We are always looking for people to write books on new and related subjects. If you have an idea for a book, please contact us at proposals@schifferbooks.com.

Other Schiffer Books on Related Subjects:
The Cycling Wangdoos by Kelly Pulley, ISBN: 978-0-7643-5406-9

This is Salty Jack.

His bedroom is a pirate ship.

Barnacle Bob came over to play.

Salty Jack said, "I'm Captain!
I give the orders! You're First Mate."

Scallywag Sanjay joined the crew.
Salty Jack said,
"I'm Captain! I give the orders!
You're Second Mate."

"Now we sing!" Salty Jack ordered.

"Hoist the main sail!" Salty Jack ordered.

"Haul up the anchor!
We're heading out to sea!"

The wind filled the sail and they
began to move.

The ship plowed through
the ocean waves.

Salty Jack looked through his telescope.

"It's Nautical Norman and Nelly the sea dog!

They're marooned on Skully Fang Island!"

Salty Jack shouted,
"We're coming over to rescue you!"
"Those rocks are dangerous!"
said Scallywag Sanjay.
"I'll steer around the rocks!"
said Barnacle Bob.

"Only the Captain steers the ship!"
declared Salty Jack.
Salty Jack steered the ship around
the jagged rocks. They threw a rope down to
Nautical Norman and Nelly the sea dog.

"I'm Captain! I give the orders!"
said Salty Jack.
"You're Cabin Boy and
you're Cabin Dog."

"Tie down the yardarm!
Batten down the scuttlebutt!" Salty Jack ordered.
"We're sailing away from this wretched island!"

Dolphins and flying fish darted through the
ship's wake as it sailed into the open sea.

Manta rays glided across the water, and whales leapt up from the deep.

Millie the Mermaid swam up to the ship.

"Ahoy Salty Jack!" she called.
"I'm Captain! I give the orders!" said Salty Jack.
"You're Cabin Girl!"
"I don't think so," said Millie.

"Well, I have a First Mate and a Second Mate, so you're Third Mate!" insisted Salty Jack.

"Nope," said Millie.
"Then you're the ship's cook! Go down and get us some fish sticks!" Salty Jack ordered.
"It's not gonna happen," said Millie as she pushed away from the ship.

"But I'm Captain!
I give the orders!"

"Mermaids don't take orders,"
Millie said and waved goodbye.
Salty Jack was furious.

"Can I steer the ship?" Barnacle Bob asked. Salty Jack shouted, "Sea Slugs and Squid Guts! Only the Captain gets to steer the ship! Go swab the quarterdeck!"

"Let's follow my map to Pirate Plunderbum's lost treasure!" said Scallywag Sanjay. "Lobster Claws and Flounder Fuzz!" Salty Jack hollered. "On MY ship we use MY maps!"

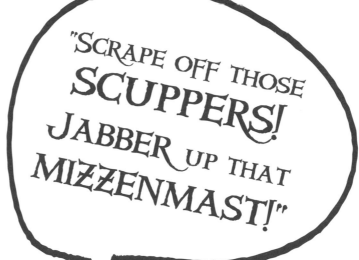

Salty Jack **BELLOWED!**

Salty Jack **BOOMED!**

Salty Jack **BARKED,**

BLUSTERED, and **BRAYED!**

Barnacle Bob, Scallywag Sanjay, and Nautical Norman decided to abandon ship. "We'll see you later, Jack," they said as they walked down the gangplank. Nelly the sea dog followed close behind.

"You can't just walk off the ship!
We're in the middle of the ocean!"

Salty Jack sailed on alone.
He swabbed the quarterdeck.

He tightened up the jibberboom.
But it wasn't very much fun.

Millie the Mermaid swam up from below. "What happened to your crew?" she asked.

"Mutiny," said Salty Jack.

"I was having so much fun. Then they ruined it."

"Were they having fun?" asked Millie.

Salty Jack didn't answer.

Millie swam away. Salty Jack tried to draw a map. But he really didn't know how to draw a map.

He fell asleep to the steady beat of the rolling
waves slapping against the side of the ship.

The next day Salty Jack spied Barnacle Bob.

"Ahoy Bobby! Come on board!"
Salty Jack called out.

"Can I steer the ship?" Barnancle Bob asked.

"Of course," Salty Jack answered.

"Can I give some orders?" Barnancle Bob asked.

"Sure!" Salty Jack answered.

"SCUTTLE UP THE FLUBBER-HOIST!"

Barnacle Bob ordered.

Salty Jack hailed Scallywag Sanjay.
"Ahoy Sanjay! Time to go exploring!"

"Norman and I just made a new map. Can
we bring it?" asked Scallywag Sanjay.
"Of course," Salty Jack answered.

"We'll set sail for Dragon Rock!" Scallywag Sanjay explained. "We'll lay anchor at Scrub-a-dub Cove, next to the purple sea serpent."
"The purple sea serpent was my idea!" said Norman.

"Then we'll follow Pirate Plunderbum's footprints to the secret cave, and dig HERE!" said Scallywag Sanjay.
"Can there be a velociraptor guarding the secret cave?" asked Norman.
"Of course!" said everybody.

Scallywag Sanjay led the way to
Scrub-a-dub Cove. Barnacle Bob steered the ship.
Nautical Norman tied up the velociraptor.

Everyone helped dig up Pirate Plunderbum's lost treasure.

They all took turns giving orders
and they all had fun.

And they all sang out.

"YO HO HO! AND SCRIDDLE DEE DEE!
WE'LL SMASH THE WAVES!
WE'LL RULE THE SEA!"

THE FOLLOWING ARE WORDS THAT REAL PIRATES USED.

Salty Jack and his friends use these words too (but sometimes the wrong way).

BARNACLE: A small animal with a shell that attaches itself to the side of a ship.

BATTEN: To fasten something.

GANGPLANK: A moveable ramp that people use to walk on and off a ship.

JABBER: To talk very fast.

MAROONED: Stuck in a place where it's hard to get away.

MASTS: The big poles that stick up on a ship.

MIZZENMAST: One of the ship's masts.

MUTINY: When the sailors refuse to take orders from the captain.

NAUTICAL: Anything that relates to sailors or navigation.

QUARTERDECK: Part of the ship's deck, or floor.

SCALLYWAG: A rascal.

SCUPPER: A hole in the side of a ship for water to drain off of the deck.

SCUTTLE: To run in a hurry.

SCUTTLEBUTT: A barrel of fresh drinking water on a ship.

YARDARM: Part of the ship's yard. The yard is like a curtain rod, attached to the mast, where the sail hangs from.

THE FOLLOWING ARE NONSENSE WORDS THAT SALTY JACK AND HIS FRIENDS USE.

SCRIDDLE   PLUNDERBUM

FLUBBER-HOIST   JIBBERBOOM